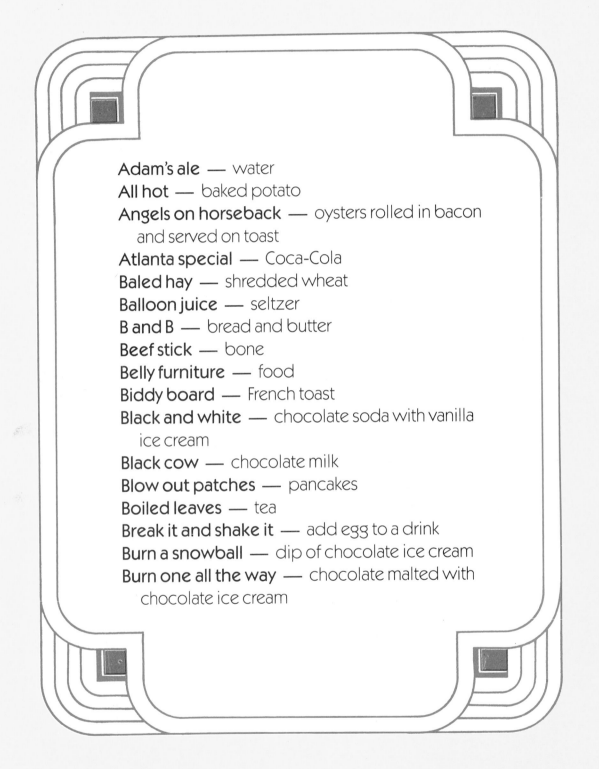

Adam's ale — water

All hot — baked potato

Angels on horseback — oysters rolled in bacon and served on toast

Atlanta special — Coca-Cola

Baled hay — shredded wheat

Balloon juice — seltzer

B and B — bread and butter

Beef stick — bone

Belly furniture — food

Biddy board — French toast

Black and white — chocolate soda with vanilla ice cream

Black cow — chocolate milk

Blow out patches — pancakes

Boiled leaves — tea

Break it and shake it — add egg to a drink

Burn a snowball — dip of chocolate ice cream

Burn one all the way — chocolate malted with chocolate ice cream

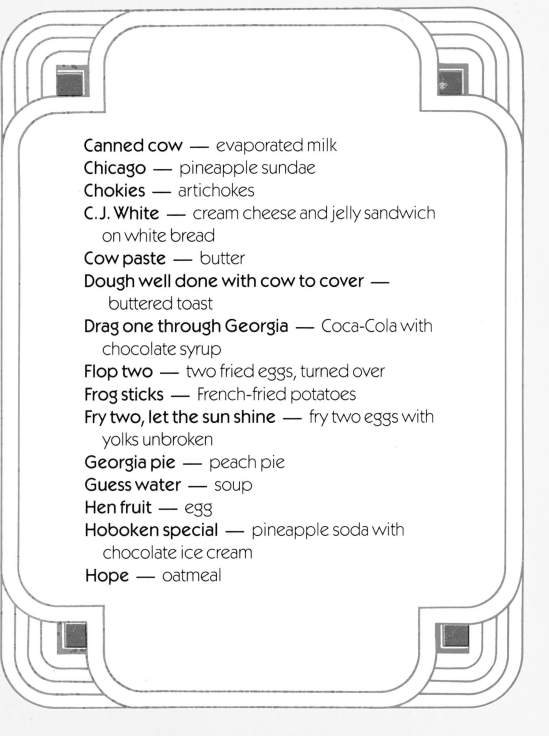

Canned cow — evaporated milk

Chicago — pineapple sundae

Chokies — artichokes

C.J. White — cream cheese and jelly sandwich
on white bread

Cow paste — butter

Dough well done with cow to cover —
buttered toast

Drag one through Georgia — Coca-Cola with
chocolate syrup

Flop two — two fried eggs, turned over

Frog sticks — French-fried potatoes

Fry two, let the sun shine — fry two eggs with
yolks unbroken

Georgia pie — peach pie

Guess water — soup

Hen fruit — egg

Hoboken special — pineapple soda with
chocolate ice cream

Hope — oatmeal

FRANK AND ERNEST

FRANK AND ERNEST

by Alexandra Day

SCHOLASTIC INC.

New York Toronto London Auckland Sydney

ISBN 0-590-41556-5

12 11 10 9 8 7 6 5 4 3 2   3   1 2 3 4 5 6/9

Printed in the U.S.A.   08

"This looks like just what I need."

"I'll only be gone three days, but my diner is very important to me. I hope you can handle it."

"Don't worry, Mrs. Miller. We will take as good care of it as you would."

"Look here, Ernest. Diners have a language of their own, and we will need to learn it before we can wait on people."

"It's really beautiful, Frank. It will be great fun doing this job, but I think it will also be a huge challenge."

"I'll take a hamburger with lettuce, tomato, and an onion."

"Hey, Frank, burn one,
take it through the garden,
and pin a rose on it."

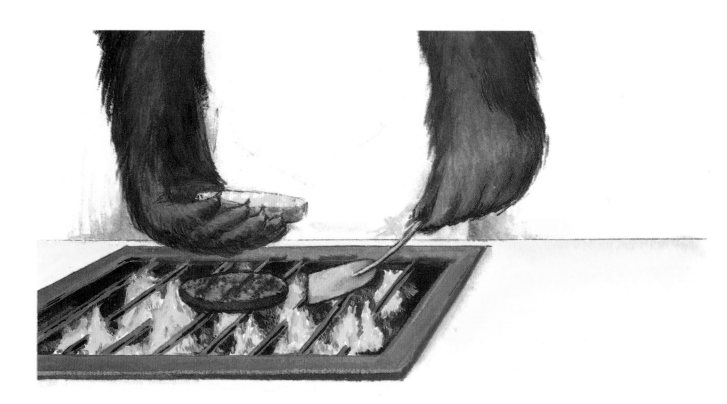

"I'd like a piece
of apple pie and
a glass of milk, please."

"Eve with a lid and moo juice, Ernest."

"A hot dog with ketchup
for Jimmy, and a serving
of Jell-O for me,
if you please."

"Paint a bow-wow red, Frank,
and I need a nervous pudding."

"Well, Ernest, we made it through the first day."

"Gimme a vanilla milk shake with an egg in it, to go."

"Would you give me a hand, Ernest? I need a white cow — make it cackle and let it walk."

"I'll take the pancakes with maple syrup,
and coffee with cream and sugar."

"A stack with Vermont
and a blonde with sand."

"I think we're getting better at this, Ernest."

"May I have an English muffin
with butter, and a cup of
black coffee, please?"

"Burn the British, cow to cover, and draw one in the dark."

"A tuna sandwich on toast, please,
and a Dr. Pepper with the ice left out."

"Ernest, I need a radio sandwich
down, and an M.D.,
hold the hail."

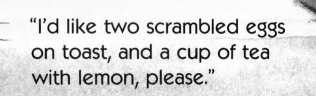

"I'd like two scrambled eggs
on toast, and a cup of tea
with lemon, please."

"Adam and Eve on a raft, wreck'em, and a spot with a twist."

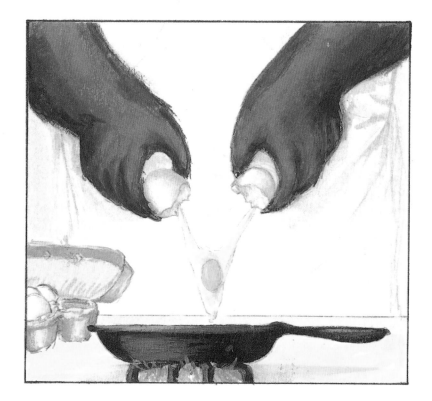

"Well, we did it!"

"Gentlemen, the place looks beautiful, and I've heard nothing but good things from my friends who ate here in the last few days. You did a fine job, and I'll recommend your services to everyone I know."

Hot one — bowl of chili

Hot top — hot chocolate

Hounds on an island — frankfurters and beans

Houseboat — banana split

Hug one — glass of orange juice

Ice on rice — rice pudding with ice cream

Life preservers — doughnuts

Lighthouse — bottle of catsup

L.T. — lettuce and tomato sandwich

Mama on a raft — marmalade on toast

Mats — pancakes

Mike and Ike — salt and pepper shakers

Million on a platter — plate of baked beans

Mississippi mud — mustard

Oh gee — orange juice

One from the Alps — Swiss cheese sandwich

Pink stick — strawberry ice cream

Popeye — spinach

Put a hat on it — add ice cream

Put out the lights and cry — order of liver and onions

Rabbit food — lettuce
Raft — slice of toast
Shake one in the hay — strawberry milk shake
Shivering Eve — apple jelly
Sneeze — pepper
Splash of red noise — bowl of tomato soup
Splash out of the garden — bowl of vegetable soup
Sun kiss — orange juice
Sweep the kitchen — plate of hash
Throw it in the mud — add chocolate syrup
Twist it, choke it, and make it cackle — egg chocolate malted milk shake
Vermont — maple syrup
Wart — olive
Wax — American cheese
Wimpy — hamburger
Wrecked hen fruit — scrambled eggs
Yellow paint — mustard
Yum-yum — sugar